I'M A DUCK!

Story and pictures by
TERI SLOAT

G. P. PUTNAM'S SONS

G. P. PUTNAM'S SONS

A division of Penguin Young Readers Group.

Published by The Penguin Group. Penguin Group (USA) Inc.,

375 Hudson Street, New York, NY 10014, U.S.A.

Penguin Group (Canada), 90 Eglinton Avenue East, Suite 700,

Toronto, Ontario, Canada M4P 2Y3 (a division of Pearson Penguin

Canada Inc.). Penguin Books Ltd, 80 Strand, London WC2R 0RL, England.

Penguin Ireland, 25 St. Stephen's Green, Dublin 2, Ireland (a division of Penguin

Books Ltd.). Penguin Group (Australia), 250 Camberwell Road, Camberwell,

Victoria 3124, Australia (a division of Pearson Australia Group Pty Ltd).

Penguin Books India Pvt Ltd, 11 Community Centre, Panchsheel Park, New Delhi

- 110 017, India. Penguin Group (NZ), Cnr Airborne and Rosedale Roads, Albany,

Auckland 1310, New Zealand (a division of Pearson New Zealand Ltd). Penguin Books

(South Africa) (Pty) Ltd, 24 Sturdee Avenue, Rosebank, Johannesburg 2196, South Africa.

Penguin Books Ltd, Registered Offices: 80 Strand, London WC2R 0RL, England.

Published simultaneously in Canada. Manufactured in China by South China Printing Co. Ltd. Design by Gunta Alexander.
Text set in Stone Informal. The art is done with pastel on Winsor & Newton 140 lb. cold press watercolor paper.

Library of Congress Cataloging-in-Publication Data

Sloat, Teri. I'm a duck! / Teri Sloat. p. cm. Summary: A duck marvels at how wonderful it is to be a duck, with feathers, webbed feet,
and wings that can fly, from the time he is hatched until he becomes a dad. [1. Ducks—Fiction. 2. Stories in rhyme.] I. Title: I am a duck!.
II. Title. PZ8.3.S63245Im 2006 [E]—dc22 2004020479 ISBN 0-399-24274-0 10 9 8 7 6 5 4 3 2 1 First Impression

*T*o the happy mallard
and his family
at the Rohnert Park Doubletree Hotel.

Duck?

Yup, you're a duck!

I'm a duck.

Yup,
  by some magnificent
  stroke of good luck,

I'm a duck!

Not only that,
I can quack.
It gives me a thrill
when I open my bill
and I **QUACK!**

QUA

QUA-A

QUA-A-ACK

Look at these feet—

pretty neat!

Wow.

They're webbed.

What a treat!

I can waddle around,

    paddle upstream and down.

Watch me walk through the mud.
I make tracks!
It gives me a thrill so I open my bill
and I quack!

And wings—I've got **wings!**
Just think, I grew both of these things!

I can flap.

I can fly . . .

I can soar through the sky.

When I coast in to land,
   it's outstanding. It's grand!

It gives me a thrill
   so I open my bill
      and I QUACK!

But wait. . . .

What's that quacking back?

What are the odds,

       the chances,

              the luck?

Coming in for a landing by me is a . . . duck?

Yup. A duck!

And here's what's making
my mallard tail curl—
the duck landing next to me
is a . . . girl!

She has freckled feathers,

two wings, and webbed feet!

She's amazing . . . she's graceful . . . a pleasure to meet.

There's a strut in my waddle now.
I've got a wife!

I tell you, this girl has changed my whole life.

She thinks I'm the best.
I can tell she's impressed.
And I've found an incredible spot
for our nest.

Spring's in the air. Life couldn't be better.

But wait, what's she doing?

She's plucking a feather!

First one, then another, right out of her chest.

She's saying it's time to feather our nest.

Now look what she's doing.

One...

Two...

Three...

She's bending her legs.

Four...

Five...

Six...

Seven...

Eight...

No stopping her now—

Nine...

TEN!

SHE'S LAYING **EGGS!**

Wow! Ten perfect eggs. Not one single crack!

It gives me a thrill so I open my bill

and I QUACK!

She quacks back!

By some magnificent stroke of good luck,

we're both ducks—

lucky ducks!

She fluffs herself out, sits folding her legs.

She talks about babies hatching from eggs.

It's making me nervous.

I'm coming unglued.

She's quacking at me.

She says she needs **food.**

I'm hunting down snails,
    polliwogs,
       and small fish.
I'm granting
my beautiful wife
   every wish.

MORE!

I wish she would stand
    and stretch out her legs.

I'm dying to see what's
inside of those eggs!

Today's the big day!
I see beaks peeking through!
I'm feeling faint . . .
could it be true?

By some magnificent
stroke of good luck,
inside of every
egg is a . . .
DUCK?

Yup,
they're all
DUCKS!

Look at those wings,
     those perfect webbed feet.

And their tracks are so tiny. Isn't that sweet?
It gives me a thrill so I open my bill
and I QUACK!
Hear that? **They quack back.**
They're all ducks!

Of all the magnificent luck
that I've had,
nothing beats being a duck and a . . .

...DAD!